Also by Heide Stöllinger and Adelheid Dahimène
Donkeys (Gecko Press 2005)
By Heide Stöllinger and Klara Fall
Elfrida (Gecko Press 2006)

Original title: *Wir und das neue Tier*
© 2008 Residenz Verlag
im Niederösterreichischen Pressehaus
Druck- und Verlagsgesellschaft mbH
St. Pölten – Salzburg
All rights reserved

This edition first published in Australia and New Zealand in 2008 by Gecko Press
PO Box 9335, Marion Square, Wellington 6141, New Zealand
Email: info@geckopress.com

© Gecko Press 2008

Thanks to Miriam Tornquist and Johannes Contag for their help with translation.

National Library of New Zealand Cataloguing-in-Publication Data
is available for this title.

Typesetting: Archetype, Wellington
Printing: Everbest, China

ISBN paperback: 978-1-877467-06-6
ISBN hardback: 978-1-877467-05-9

For more curiously good books, please visit www.geckopress.com

Adelheid Dahimène

Illustrated by Heide Stöllinger

Making Friends

GECKO PRESS

The sun was beaming and the sky was smiling.
Dog was growling and Pig was grunting.

Rooster crowed and Mouse squealed.
Cat yowled and Goat bleated.

Dog growled that he was bored with the others. He told Pig, 'I'm sick of the way you roll around in the mud all day. You never come up with anything fresh.'

Pig grunted at Rooster's vanity, 'Quit crowing about yourself.
We've heard it all before.'

Goat bleated about the fuss Cat was making. 'Go and see how you like cow's milk if mine's not good enough. Cows only eat *grass*.'

Mouse squealed when Dog stood on her tail — again. 'You always pick on the underdog. Show some consideration for size.'

As the animals snitched and bickered, a pigeon flew into the farmyard.

'Have you brought us something?' Pig put on a friendly voice.
'We could do with a change around here — a new friend,
for instance.'

'Make one yourselves, then,' the pigeon
cooed, and flew back out into the big
wide world.

'Let's get to work,' crowed Rooster, 'and see if we can make a brand new friend.'

Cat found string. Mouse sneaked cheese from the kitchen while
Dog dug up his old bones. Goat rolled a pumpkin
into the yard, Pig hauled straw from his sty,
and Rooster scratched about for feathers.

They bound the straw with string and pushed bones in at the ends. The pumpkin would go on top once they'd stuck down the cheese with lots of spit.

The new friend just sat there.

'Ask it if it feels okay,' said Goat.
'Are you all right?' whispered Cat.

The friend said nothing.

'It's as boring as you are,' Dog told Pig.
'It must be scared of us,' said Rooster. 'We need to
make a better impression. Let's show it our very best selves.'

Pig went up and laid her snout on their new friend's front.
She sucked in hard. Five or ten fleas in one go!

Goat offered healing herbs from the field, in case their
friend had a tummy-ache.

Rooster spread his wings and crooned a lullaby.

Dog put on his fiercest guard-dog face.

Cat licked clean their friend's new straw coat.

Mouse twitched her clever nose and read aloud from a magazine:
'New friends are sometimes found in the most unlikely places.'

They all cheered and clapped.
But still their new friend said nothing.

'We can't have put it together properly,' Dog said to Goat. 'But maybe your herbs would fix my toothache.'

'I had no idea how good you are at cleaning,' Pig told Cat. 'No chance you could make an old pig pink again, I suppose?'

'That lullaby was bliss,' said Goat. 'Will you sing for me some evening? I find it so hard to fall asleep.'

Mouse told Dog: 'With you guarding us, even the stars tremble.'

'You're not just a layabout, after all,' Cat purred to Pig. 'Even *my* fleas couldn't hold out against that snout.'

'How clever you are,' Rooster told Mouse. 'Such fine reading with such tiny eyes. I'm mighty impressed.'

'Friends *do* turn up in unlikely places,' Goat said to Pig.
'Yes,' said Pig. 'Shall we dance the pig trot?'